LOOKOUT
POINT

CHARITY

THE ILAS

LADYFACE

LABYRINTH

ILA VISTA

GENERAL STORE

Toys

CANDY

PARADISE
COVE

KNOTTY PINE

SCHOOL HOUSE

FIRESIDE

Welcome to the
World of

WW ™

WANDERING
ROAD

WILLOWBE WOODS
Campfire Stories

The Not Me Monster

Written by
Ila Wallen

Illustrated by
Robert Sauber

Willowbe Woods Campfire Stories
Created by
Bill Wallen & Ila Wallen

BENT WILLOW
PUBLISHING

BENT WILLOW
PUBLISHING

2260 Townsgate Road Suite #2
Westlake Village, CA 91361
(805) 381-1033
www.bentwillowpublishing.com

The Not Me Monster

Bill Wallen - Publisher & Art Director • Michael Wallen - Designer • Rich Conturo - Graphic Art Production
Patrick Davidson - Editorial Director • Carolyn Wallen and Christine Oliver - Editors

The Willowbe Woods Campfire Stories
Created by
Bill Wallen & Ila Wallen

Printed in the United States by Phoenix Color, Rockaway, N. J.
10 9 8 7 6 5 4 3 2 1

Publisher's Cataloging-in-Publication

Wallen, Ila
The not me monster / written by Ila Wallen;
illustrated by Robert Sauber ; created by Bill Wallen &
Ila Wallen. – 1st ed.
p. cm. – (Willowbe Woods Campfire Stories ; 2)

SUMMARY: Bunny's embarrased because she made a
mistake, so she fibs and blames a "monster." Soon she
learns that making a mistake is okay, but fibbing to her
friends is not.
Audience: Ages 2-8
ISBN 0-9710627-1-4

1. Monsters -- Juvenile fiction. 2. Honesty -- Juvenile
fiction. [1. Monsters -- Fiction. 2. Honesty -- Fiction.
3. Stories in rhyme] I. Sauber, Robert, ill. II.
Wallen, Bill. III. Title.

PZ8.3.W175No 2002   [E] - QB102-578

To Giancarlo:
I wish you enough.
- Ila Wallen

To my daughter, Sophia Zoe:
a source of Wisdom and Life.
- Robert Sauber

Take my hand and follow me,
To the enchanted woods of Willowbe.
Laughter and warmth surround the campfire,
In Willowbe Woods, where stories inspire.

Papa Rango greets friends from far and near
With happy hugs and a welcoming cheer.

The Willowbeings gather at twilight,
 Sharing stories by the campfire light.
Papa Rango opens his book with care,
 And asks, "Tonight, whose story shall I share?"

There are yells and screams and shrieks galore
    As if they'd never been asked this question before.

From around the tree all the kids cry loud,
    But only one voice stands out from the crowd.

It's Bunny's, the rabbit, her voice full of cheer.
"Me, Me, Me," she yells, grinning from ear to ear.
"Remember when a monster made a mess of our day,
And I was the one who helped send it away?"

"What a wonderful choice," Papa Rango says with delight.
"Here we go, let me start; Once upon a Willowbe Night . . ."

The Willowbeings were planning a party for a friend.
It was a birthday surprise and all would attend.
Bunny volunteered to make a sign for the door,
And promised she wouldn't get paint on the floor.

Just as Bunny finished the Happy Birthday sign,
She accidentally spilled paint on her design.
"Oh noodles," said Bunny. "Look what I've done."
"What happened here?" Sophie asked everyone.

Her friends were pointing their fingers at Bunny.
The looks on their faces made her tummy feel funny.

She didn't know what to do, or what should be said;
Then a silly idea popped into her head.

"Did you see the monster that spilled all the paint?
With its long purple tail, I wanted to faint.
It has crooked teeth that are too big for its face.
It scared me," said Bunny, "then ran out of the place."

"A monster in Willowbe!" Bandit started to yell.
"With green hairy arms!" said Bunny. "And a horrible smell!"
Will asked, "Does he have eighteen toes and three feet?
That's definitely something I don't want to meet."

Everyone laughed and forgot about the monster real soon.
Then Flynn asked Bunny to help him blow up balloons.

Bunny's balloon wouldn't tie in a knot.

It stretched.

It snapped.

Ouch! Her finger got caught.

PHLOOP PHEEWW SPITTER SPATT

...her balloon took off in flight.

It flipped and it dived,
hitting all in its sight.

Knocking over the
piñata and spilling
candy to the floor,

The balloon splashed
in the fruit punch,

Then it whizzed out
the door.

"BUNNY," her friends yelled.
   Their voices rang in her ears.
"It's not me! It's not me!"
   Her eyes filled with tears.

So Bunny blamed the monster
   she'd made up in her head,
When she should have
   admitted her mistake instead.

Bunny went outside to see what else could be done,
And saw Will frosting the cake. Ooh, it looked fun!
"I can help Will put candles on the cake.
That's something I know I can do and can't break."

Though she tried and tried with her high rabbit hop,
Bunny couldn't quite reach the cake's tippy top.
She stretched really tall, tilting this way and that.
"WHOAHH!" She fell into the cake with a gigantic splat!

Upset by all that had happened that day,
Bunny ran to Mystic Lake to get far, far away.

She looked in the water and what did she see?
"Ahhhh, a monster!
Hey wait, that's just little old me."

Bunny went to Charity
for advice on what to do,
Mentioning her little fib
that grew, grew, and grew.

"I didn't tell the truth
and now all my friends are afraid.
Charity, can you help me with
the huge mistake I made?"

"Mistakes happen all the time,"
Charity said with certainty,
"And correcting them is easy
with a little honesty."

"To help your friends feel better, you should apologize.
I have an idea that could work but we need a disguise."

Later that day, a mysterious figure stood tall.
  "I'm sorry," a voice grumbled, "for my trouble, big and small,
For the mess I made with the paint, balloons and cake.
  I'm really no monster . . ."

". . . I'm Bunny, and I made a mistake.

I was embarrassed about
all the trouble I caused,
So I made up the monster
to cover for my flaws.

I learned that mistakes happen,
That's how you learn about you.
But it's wrong to fib about
things that you do."

Bunny's friends hugged her tight and said it was okay.
They each admitted making their own mistakes that day.
"Well," said Bunny, "let's get this party looking just right.
Remember, there's a birthday taking place here tonight."

There was a glimmering shimmer in Bunny's big eyes
    As she squealed out in laughter a loud Willowbe, "Surprise!"

By telling the truth, now nothing was wrong.
    And Bunny's friends joined her
    in a grand birthday song.